June Kirkpatrick

The Little Church Mouse of the Loretto Chapel

By June Kirkpatrick

Illustrated by Michele M.K. Brokaw

Gently Worded Books

The Little Church Mouse of the Loretto Chapel
Copyright © 2000

ISBN 0-9708940-1-5 (previously ISBN 1-929115-02-4)

LCCN 00-107739

Text © June Kirkpatrick

Illustrations © Michele M.K. Brokaw

Second Printing 2001

Printed in the USA
Starline Printing
Albuqueruqe, NM

*This book is dedicated to the
Sisters of Loretto.
Without their courage,
sacrifices, faith, and prayers,
The Chapel of Our Lady of Light
(The Loretto Chapel)
would never have been built.*

All was quiet in
the small stone
chapel on this
joyous Christmas
eve.
   The only sound
was of four small
feet scurrying
across the chapel
floor.

A little church mouse peeked over one of the wooden pews. His small grey ears twitched back and forth and his big dark eyes filled with tears.

On the eve of the celebration of the Christ Child's coming, he was all alone.

The little church mouse had a thought. He curled up at the feet of one of the archangels and silently prayed, hoping this angel of such high rank would listen to his humble request - not to be alone on this holiest of nights.

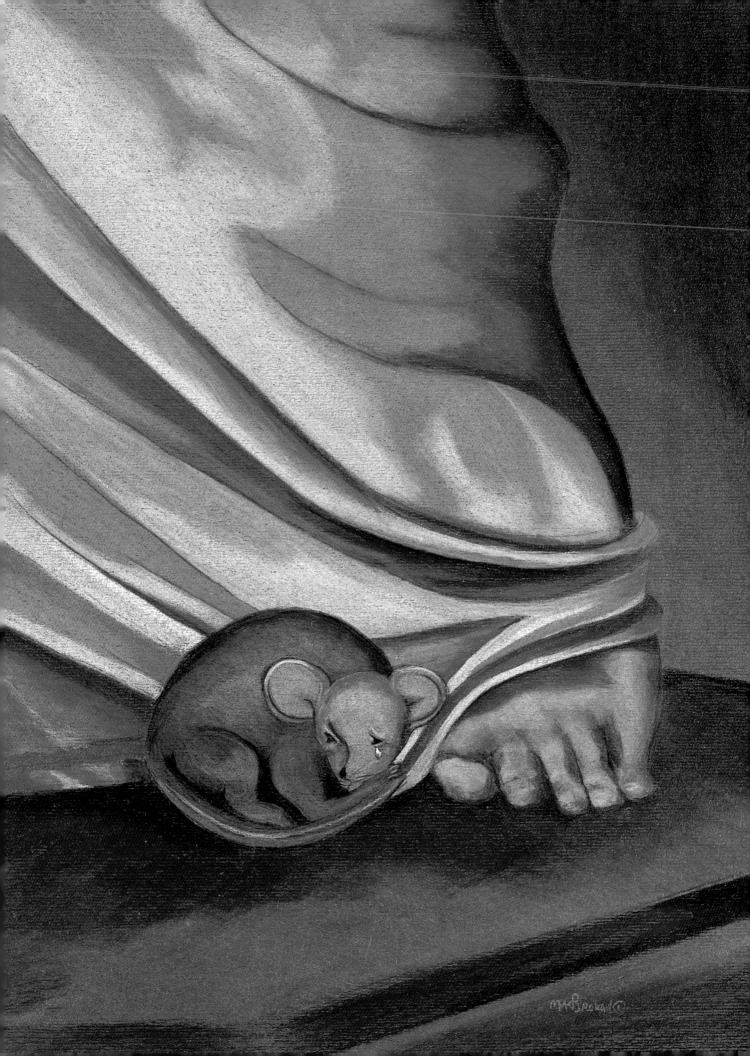

As he slowly lifted his head, he could not believe what he saw. The domed ceiling was filled with a golden glow as a graceful white dove flew overhead, taking in all the beauty of this small chapel that the Sisters of Loretto had struggled to build many years ago.

The dove floated
gracefully past the
eight stained glass
windows, while the
little mouse sat
quietly, perched on
the altar railing
below.

"Wait! Don't leave!" called the little mouse to the dove that was flying in the direction of the large wooden doors at the front of the chapel.

Turning quickly at the sound of this soft voice, the dove settled on the lower steps of the miraculous stairway. The dove glanced up the winding stairs at the choir loft above.

Offering words of
peace, love and friend-
ship, the little mouse
jumped from the railing
and raced over to the
resting dove.

As they sat together, the little mouse told the dove about the Sisters of Loretto and their prayers to St. Joseph, the patron saint of carpenters. The Sisters needed a staircase, which had been forgotten when the chapel was built.

"As the story goes," said the mouse, "one day a grey-haired man on a donkey came to the chapel door and asked the Sisters if he could help build their staircase to the choir loft. Using only a hammer, saw, and T-square, he built what is now regarded as a master-piece of beauty."

The mouse continued: "It took this caring man less than a year to finish the staircase, and as mysteriously as he had come, he left, without asking for pay for his work or for the wood he had used."

Several years later the railing, which is also considered a work of art, was added for the Sisters' safety.

As they sat together looking at the
beauty all around them, the large,
wooden front doors of the chapel
opened slowly.

Hearing this, the dove quickly flew up to the choir loft and landed on the wooden railing. The little church mouse could not climb the narrow, wooden, spiral staircase's thirty-three steps, so he used

the railing as his
winding road up.
he joined his new-
found friend and
they watched the
people as they
gathered in the
chapel below.

The once-quiet chapel was now filled with laughter, songs, and prayers of the holiday season.

The little church mouse and the dove joined in singing the Christmas carols. Their sweet voices rose up to heaven as they sang about the Little Lord Jesus asleep in the hay.

A-WAY IN A MAN-GER NO CRIB FOR A BED THE LIT-TLE LORD JE-SUS LAID DOWN HIS SWEET HEAD THE STARS IN THE SKY

Tonight was a special night, a night of miracles. The little church mouse had been very unhappy but now his eyes sparkled with happiness.

He was not alone.

We wish you peace o

...arth, good will to all.

June Kirkpatrick has always enjoyed the art of storytelling to her children and now to her grandchildren, be it real life or fantasy. A long-time New Mexican, she lives in Santa Fe with her husband Charles and a variety of animals. The Loretto Chapel (The Chapel of our Lady of Light) and the Sisters of Loretto were her inspiration for writing this Christmas tale.

This is June's second book. Her first book was *Barn Kitty*.

The Photography Studio

All of the author's and illustrator's royalties will be donated to the Sisters of Loretto.

Michele M.K. Brokaw's award-winning colored pencil paintings are part of several private and corporate collections. The Loretto Chapel remains one of her favorite subjects, and she finds continuing inspiration in the details found in its beauty. Michele lives and works in Santa Fe, N.M., with her husband Bill. They are surrounded by their loving children, grandchildren, and extended family, including the Loretto Chapel dove.

To the family.
Michele M.K. Brokaw

Blue Rose Photography